THE INFINITY RAINBOW CLUB

VIOLET AND THE JURASSIC LAND EXHIBIT

BY **JEN MALIA**

ILLUSTRATED BY **PETER FRA** 'S

beaming ☀

For my parents and grandma who took me
to the Carnegie Museum of Natural History
more times than I can remember—JM

To all those that inspire and nurture the best
in ourselves—PF

29 28 27 26 25 24 23   1 2 3 4 5 6 7 8 9

Hardcover ISBN: 978-1-5064-8597-3
Paperback ISBN: 978-1-5064-9342-8
eBook ISBN: 978-1-5064-8598-0

Library of Congress Cataloging-in-Publication Data

Names: Malia, Jen, author. | Francis, Peter, illustrator.
Title: Violet and the Jurassic Land exhibit / by Jen Malia ; illustrated by
   Peter Francis.
Description: Minneapolis, MN : Beaming Books, 2023 | Series: The Infinity
   Rainbow Club | Audience: Grades 4-6. | Summary: Violet navigates her OCD
   while volunteering at the local natural history museum.
Identifiers: LCCN 2023009147 (print) | LCCN 2023009148 (ebook) | ISBN
   9781506485973 (hardback) | ISBN 9781506493428 (paperback) | ISBN
   9781506485980 (ebook)
Subjects: LCAC: Obsessive-compulsive disorder--Fiction. |
   Paleontology--Fiction. | Clubs--Fiction. | Museums--Fiction. | Chinese
   Americans--Fiction.
Classification: LCC PZ7.1.M34696 Vi 2023 (print) | LCC PZ7.1.M34696
   (ebook) | DDC [Fic]--dc23
LC record available at https://lccn.loc.gov/2023009147
LC ebook record available at https://lccn.loc.gov/2023009148

Hardcover: 63471506485973; MAY2023
Paperback: 63471506493428; MAY2023

Beaming Books
PO Box 1209
Minneapolis, MN 55
Beamingbooks.com

THE INFINITY RAINBOW CLUB

VIOLET AND THE JURASSIC LAND EXHIBIT

BY **JEN MALIA**

ILLUSTRATED BY **PETER FRANCIS**

beaming books

MINNEAPOLIS

**For my parents and grandma who took me
to the Carnegie Museum of Natural History
more times than I can remember—JM**

**To all those that inspire and nurture the best
in ourselves—PF**

29 28 27 26 25 24 23   1 2 3 4 5 6 7 8 9

Hardcover ISBN: 978-1-5064-8597-3
Paperback ISBN: 978-1-5064-9342-8
eBook ISBN: 978-1-5064-8598-0

Library of Congress Cataloging-in-Publication Data

Names: Malia, Jen, author. | Francis, Peter, illustrator.
Title: Violet and the Jurassic Land exhibit / by Jen Malia ; illustrated by
   Peter Francis.
Description: Minneapolis, MN : Beaming Books, 2023 | Series: The Infinity
   Rainbow Club | Audience: Grades 4-6. | Summary: Violet navigates her OCD
   while volunteering at the local natural history museum.
Identifiers: LCCN 2023009147 (print) | LCCN 2023009148 (ebook) | ISBN
   9781506485973 (hardback) | ISBN 9781506493428 (paperback) | ISBN
   9781506485980 (ebook)
Subjects: CYAC: Obsessive-compulsive disorder--Fiction. |
   Paleontology--Fiction. | Clubs--Fiction. | Museums--Fiction. | Chinese
   Americans--Fiction.
Classification: LCC PZ7.1.M34696 Vi 2023 (print) | LCC PZ7.1.M34696
   (ebook) | DDC [Fic]--dc23
LC record available at https://lccn.loc.gov/2023009147
LC ebook record available at https://lccn.loc.gov/2023009148

Hardcover: 63474; 9781506485973; MAY2023
Paperback: 63474; 9781506493428; MAY2023

Beaming Books
PO Box 1209
Minneapolis, MN 55440-1209
Beamingbooks.com

CHAPTER 1

Sifting through the dark-gray clay to look for dinosaur bones calmed Violet Chen's mind and body. It was the seventh time she searched the hillside that she found a patch of white coming out of the ground. Of course she found it the seventh time she checked. After all, seven was her lucky number.

Violet had spent almost an hour at Paleo Park. She felt like an explorer on another planet. But here Violet glimpsed Maryland from more than 110 million years ago. Paleontologists like Mom called it the Cretaceous period. This was Violet's first time at Paleo Park. But she knew the steepest slopes were always the best spots to hunt for bones from when she had gone on other dinosaur digs.

"Do you see it too?" asked Violet.

"Uh huh," said her fourth-grade classmate Nick. He flapped his hands like he always did when he was excited. Nick was in the Infinity Rainbow Club with Violet. He had started the after-school club for kids who felt different, like he did. Ms. Daisy, their special education teacher, was in charge of the club. She had arranged for the whole club and their families to come on a field trip to Paleo Park this weekend.

For the dig, Ms. Daisy had assigned Violet and Nick as partners. They bent down on opposite sides of the fossil. Violet took her field notebook out of her backpack. Ribbon bookmarks divided her notebook into different sections. Each of the seven ribbons was a different color of the rainbow. She opened her notebook to the dinosaur dig section in the middle and started a new entry.

December 8
Paleo Park
Specimen #1

1. Far back corner of the park, halfway up the hillside
2. Whitish-gray object, quarter size
3. Found near gray clay, ironstone, lignite

Violet put her green ribbon bookmark on the page and closed the field notebook.

Violet and Nick used their paintbrushes on the fossil to clear away the ironstone pebbles the way Ms. Daisy had showed them. The lignite, or small chunks of fossilized wood pieces, crumbled into an ashy powder with each brushstroke. Rubbing their work gloves gently on the fossil removed most of the sticky clay from it. It was the size of a football! Violet hadn't found a fossil *this* big before.

The rounded surface with little holes reminded Violet of a sponge. And she knew what that meant. Bone. *It has to be a dinosaur bone*, she thought.

Violet opened her field notebook to the page marked with a green ribbon. She sketched the exposed part of the fossil. Below her drawing, she continued her list of seven:

4. Spongy, football-sized
5. Appears to be a dinosaur bone

Violet cupped her hands around her mouth. "Lao Lao!"

Near the bottom of the hill, Lao Lao knelt on a thick foam pad and combed through the ground. Her silver hair peeked out of her straw hat. When Lao Lao looked up at her, Violet motioned for her to come up the hill.

"Coming!" Lao Lao yelled back.

"Your grandma makes it look easy to climb," said Nick.

Lao Lao moved at a steady pace, swinging her kneeling pad in one hand and her water bottle in the other.

Violet nodded and smiled. "She does this a lot."

When Lao Lao reached Violet and Nick, she hovered over the fossil. "Now that's a *big* dinosaur bone."

Violet was so excited. *If Lao Lao says it's a dinosaur bone,* thought Violet, *then it's a dinosaur bone.* Lao Lao was never wrong. She didn't hunt for them as part of her job, like Mom, but Lao Lao knew bones.

"I'll get Mom and Dr. Hart," said Violet. "Will you stay here with Nick and our fossil find?"

"Of course." Lao Lao knelt on her foam pad beside the fossil.

Violet scrambled up the hillside. She took seven steps. And then seven more steps. But her hiking boots lost their grip before she made it to the top.

"Ahhhh!" Violet slid backward down the hill. But one of her boots hit a large clump of rusty ironstone sticking out of the clay. She fell forward, reaching one hand out to catch herself from falling all the way to the ground. She took a deep breath in, counting to seven. And a deep breath out, counting to seven.

"Are you okay?" yelled Lao Lao behind Violet. Nick and Lao Lao were the only ones on the hillside. The only ones who would've seen her.

Violet turned around toward them.

"Yeah, I'm okay," she yelled back. Violet wished Lao Lao and Nick hadn't seen that. Not that they would make fun of her. But still, it was embarrassing.

Violet climbed the hill again, carefully calculating each step. But she imagined that she slid down the hill again and the large clump of bronze poking out of the ground didn't stop her. In her mind, she tumbled down the hillside until she ran into Lao Lao and Nick. She could picture herself breaking Lao Lao's arm and Nick's leg so that pieces of bone popped out of their skin. This was what Mom called an intrusive or unwanted thought. Violet didn't want people to get hurt. But she couldn't help imagining that they did.

When Violet imagined bad things happening to her family and friends, she told herself that the bad things hadn't actually happened. And they weren't more likely to happen just because she thought about them either. Dad had said she shouldn't try to stop the thoughts because that could make them even worse. She didn't want to let her obsessive-compulsive disorder take over. For Violet, OCD made her anxious or scary thoughts get stuck in her head, and she would repeatedly carry out rituals like making lists of seven or checking for mistakes.

Violet wasn't going to let a fall on the hillside stop her. The fossil she had found with Nick had been waiting at least 110 million years for them to discover it. Mom and Dr. Hart would know what kind of dinosaur it was. Once Violet got to the top of the hill, she took seven deep breaths. She had *made* it.

Violet scanned the crowd on the other side of the dig site. Mom's cranberry fleece jacket stood out in the distance. The kid with the chocolate-brown baseball cap hunched over the ground next to Mom was Violet's younger brother, Bo.

And not too far from them was Dad. He was hard to miss with his waterproof rainforest-ready pants and jacket. Violet walked toward them like she was on a mission. But she didn't run. The rule was to always walk so you didn't break the fossils.

"Mom, come quick!" yelled Violet while walking across the gentle slope of clay. Mom, Dad, and Bo met her halfway on large chunks of ironstone.

"Nick and I found something!" said Violet.

"Oh, great!" Mom's bronze hair stuck out of the gray bucket hat like ironstone poking out of the clay on the ground. "What did you find?"

"I found something too!" Bo put a piece of ironstone as big as his palm between Violet and Mom. The rusty color shined in the sun.

"That's great, Bo." Violet *was* happy for Bo. But she didn't have time for his fossil right now. Lao Lao and Nick were waiting for her. And Violet didn't want anything bad to happen to the dinosaur bone she had found with Nick.

"You didn't really look at it," said Bo. "Don't you want to see the fossil?" He held the piece of ironstone up higher so it was between Violet's and Mom's faces. "Dad says it's a ginkgo leaf." Dad would've known, since he was a botanist. The leaf impression was shaped like a fan.

"It's cool," said Violet. "But I need Mom's help."

"You can show everyone your fossil later, Bo," said Dad. "Violet needs to talk to Mom."

"We found bone!" said Violet. "The piece above ground is about"—Violet cupped her hands like she was holding them around a football—"this big. Too big to be anything other than a dinosaur bone."

Bo's mouth dropped open. Dad's eyebrows raised up, creating wrinkles on his forehead.

"It's *that* big?" Even Mom was impressed. And she was a paleontologist who worked at a natural history museum in Pittsburgh.

***

The Infinity Rainbow Club and their families gathered on the hillside to see the dinosaur bone.

"Attention, brilliant buzzing brains and families!" said Ms. Daisy. That was what she always called the kids in the club. Kids who had different brains like Violet. "As long as you stay in Paleo Park, you can leave the hillside anytime to continue looking for more fossils. With a bone this big, it will probably take a *long* time for Violet and Nick to unearth it."

Violet and Nick sat on opposite sides of the fossil surrounded by paintbrushes, trowels, scalpels, a roll of paper towels, a bucket of water, and plaster bandages. Violet couldn't stop smiling. Every time she looked at the fossil, her smile got bigger. Nick's smile was frozen on his face too. And his body shook with excitement.

Dr. Hart squatted down to the ground to look at the fossil. He was an expert on Maryland's dinosaurs and led field trips to Paleo Park. Like Mom, Dr. Hart was a paleontologist but at a natural history museum in Washington, DC. "It could be an *Astrodon johnstoni* femur." Dr. Hart rubbed his grayish-white beard. "That means thigh bone."

"*Astro* what?" Connor sat at the front of the crowd on the hillside, popping his Triceratops fidget. Violet knew that Connor focused best when he used his fidget.

"*Astrodon johnstoni*," said Violet. Before they came to Paleo Park, Mom had told her all about the fossils that had been found in Maryland. "It's the Maryland state dinosaur. It was a huge sauropod." Violet couldn't believe that the fossil they found might be from *Astrodon johnstoni*!

"What's a sauropod?" Ruby tapped her pencil on her field notebook.

"A dinosaur with a small head, long neck, elephant-like body, four huge tree-trunk-like legs, and a long tail," said Violet.

"It was also an herbivore." Nick stared at the bone as if he were talking to it.

But Violet knew that was just how he normally talked. Nick was autistic. *He'd rather look at the bone than look anyone in the eye*, thought Violet.

"A plant-eater." Violet was impressed that Nick had remembered what she told him about the dinosaurs found in Paleo Park.

In her field notebook, Violet added another item to her list:

6. Possible *Astrodon johnstoni* femur (sauropod, herbivore)

Violet knew the football-sized, grayish-white bone could be just the tip of the fossil. If it really were a femur, it could be huge! She wondered how far down the bone went into the ground. Would it be a 6-foot femur like the other one found at this dig site? Violet couldn't wait to find out.

"Before we start to dig out the fossil, we need to make sure the clay has been cleared from the edges of it," said Dr. Hart. "Can you find where the bone ends, Nick?"

"Yep." Nick brushed the fossil and traced his finger around it.

"I can double-check the edges of the bone." Violet repeated the same steps. Mom and Dr. Hart squatted down to look at them too.

"We're ready for the next step," said Dr. Hart. "We're going to slowly dig around the bone with the trowels."

But Violet worried that they hadn't checked the bone enough times. *Seven times would have been better*, she thought. Violet really wanted to say something about checking the fossil again, but she didn't want to interrupt. She took a deep breath, counting to seven. And she let it out, counting to seven again. Violet told herself that the fossil would be fine now because of her breaths.

Mom showed Violet where to position the trowel to make a wide, circular trench on one side of the bone, while Dr. Hart helped Nick do the same on the other side. The soft clay at Paleo Park made it easy to dig, even though it was almost winter. They used their scalpels to gently loosen clay from around the bone and used their brushes to remove it.

They dug until the bone stuck out a few inches from the clay. "It's time to plaster the exposed bone to protect it from breaking," said Dr. Hart.

This was Violet's favorite part. But plastering a fossil that was over 110 million years old also made her anxious. *Really* anxious. What if she made a mistake? What if Nick did? Even Mom and Dr. Hart could mess up. *We only have one chance to get this right*, thought Violet. *To get this dinosaur bone out of the ground in one piece.* Everyone was counting on her. But could she do it?

CHAPTER 2

A thick layer of white clouds covered the December sky. A cool breeze blew Violet's dark-brown hair away from her face. The plaster was ready to go on the fossil. *It's a perfect day to excavate a dinosaur bone*, thought Violet. *But digging and plastering a fossil is hard work.*

"Are we going to make a field jacket?" asked Violet.

Dr. Hart nodded and smiled. At least, Violet thought it was a smile buried under his beard. "I can tell that you've done this before."

"What's a field jacket?" asked Ruby.

"The plaster that wraps around the bone," said Violet, "and protects the fossil when it comes out of the ground and travels to the museum."

"That's right," said Mom. "Violet, do you remember how to make a field jacket?" Violet had put together field jackets on a weeklong dig with Mom in Wyoming last summer.

"Sure do," said Violet.

She put paper towels over the fossil to create a layer of protection on the surface of the bone. Nick followed

Dr. Hart's directions to brush the paper towels with water. For the next layer, they put strips of wet plaster bandages over the fossil. Violet got a whiff of ammonia from the bandages. *Eww!* She thought it smelled like the cat litter at her uncle's house.

An hour passed of digging and plastering. One by one those who had gathered around the fossil with excitement began to leave to look for more fossils. Violet and Nick took a break. Dr. Hart and Mom took over the digging. Unearthing a large femur was a big job.

Before she continued to dig, Violet took a deep breath in and rubbed the baby *Tyrannosaurus rex* tooth on her necklace seven times for luck. Mom had found it on a dig expedition in South Dakota. It was the same size as Violet's pinkie finger. She knew every groove on the otherwise smooth surface of the tooth and how it curled to a point at the end. She liked to run her finger on the tiny, jagged edges along each side of the tooth. The *T. rex* necklace went everywhere with Violet, especially on dinosaur digs.

After another hour of digging, Nick put down his trowel. "I think it's the end of the bone."

Dr. Hart crouched down and used his hand to feel the deep trench around the fossil. "It still looks like it's from

Astrodon johnstoni. But we'll have to wait for the bone to get cleaned up in the lab to know for sure." He stood up and nodded. "A very good specimen."

Mom examined the dinosaur bone. "Yes, the bone ends here. An excellent fossil!"

"What an amazing find, Violet and Nick!" said Ms. Daisy. In her field notebook, she listed the fossils the club and their families had found at Paleo Park that day.

In her own field notebook, Violet sketched the fossil in its field jacket. She added one more item to the list:

7. Femur about 2 feet long

Violet thought all her lists *had* to have seven items. Mom and Dad called this a compulsion. Violet worried that something bad would happen if she didn't make a list of seven. She wasn't supposed to keep writing them because they could make her OCD worse. But it was too hard to stop. Violet had done lists of seven for as long as she could remember. Besides, what if the list just happened to have seven items, like the one she'd just made?

Violet wasn't convinced that the femur bone was completely uncovered. She imagined Mom and Dr. Hart taking the fossil out of the ground too soon. A video

played in her head of the dinosaur bone cracking in half. *The bone must go deeper*, thought Violet. She couldn't let this go.

"Wait!" said Violet. "I want to check to make sure we uncovered all the bone." Violet placed her hand in the trench and moved gently around it. She felt for the edges of the bone. After seven times, she couldn't find any signs of the bone going any further down.

But Violet felt a small bump in the ground near the bone. She leaned her head close to the clay to get a better look at it. She was *so* close that the swampy smell from the ground filled her nose. Mom had said Paleo

Park was swampy over 110 million years ago, but Violet wasn't expecting it to smell like a swamp *now*.

She used her scalpel and brush to remove more clay from around the bump. "There!" She pointed in the trench close to the femur. "I see another bone. A much smaller bone!"

Mom peered down at the trench. "Violet is right. There *is* more bone!"

The small crowd around the fossil gasped.

Violet opened her field notebook to a new page.

Specimen #2

1. Far back corner of the park, halfway up the hillside
2. Whitish-gray tiny bone
3. Found near gray clay, ironstone, lignite
4. Below Specimen #1 in the clay

Using her scalpel and brush again, Violet uncovered a group of tiny bones. "It looks like the bones of a hatchling!"

"You mean a baby dinosaur?" Ruby bobbed her head around, trying to get a better view. Her short, red hair poked out of her hockey beanie.

Violet nodded.

Dr. Hart knelt to examine the trench. "Well, I'll be. It's a hatchling. Not the first one found in Paleo Park. But it's quite a find. Probably another *Astrodon johnstoni.*"

Ms. Daisy left to let the rest of the club and their families know about the new discovery.

In her field notebook, Violet added an "s" to item 2 on her list so that it now said "bones." Then she sketched the tiny bones of the hatchling. The neck tilted backward. The legs tangled in the clay. Below the drawing, she continued her list:

5. Possible Astrodon johnstoni (sauropod, herbivore)
6. Hatchling
7. All the hatchling bones in the space of a soccer ball

A large crowd formed around the fossil dig again. Everyone took turns looking at the hatchling bones poking out of the gray clay.

Violet checked the fossil edges of the baby dinosaur seven times. Her hand holding the trowel shook. Violet took a deep breath in, counting to seven. And a deep breath out, counting to seven. *Please, don't smash the tiny bones*, she said to herself.

Violet dug a much smaller trench around the

hatchling. The soccer ball–sized clay pedestal had the tiny hatchling bones packed in it. The 110-million-year-old bones were too delicate to remove from the clay here in the field. Violet plastered the baby dinosaur in its own field jacket. First, she put paper towels over the clay pedestal. After brushing the paper towels with water, she added the strips of wet plaster bandages.

The fossils in their field jackets had to stay in Paleo Park overnight to dry. Then Dr. Hart would send them to the natural history museum in Washington, DC. Violet wished they could go to the one in Pittsburgh instead. The museum there was her second home. A place where she would be able to see the fossils anytime.

Dr. Hart would make sure the fossil finders' names stayed with the fossils in the official record. Violet and Nick's dinosaur femur, Violet's hatchling, and Bo's ginkgo leaf impression weren't the only fossils found that day. Nick's older sister, Haley, had found what Dr. Hart thought was a *Dromaeosaur* tooth. He said *Dromaeosaur* was a small, feathered, meat-eating dinosaur that walked on its back legs. A fifth grader named Matt had uncovered a crocodile tooth. He was the oldest in the club. Jasmine's little sister, Destiny, had dug up a sequoia cone. And Connor's little brother, Luke, had unearthed a turtle shell.

***

After a picnic lunch, the club and their families gathered in the interpretive garden near the dinosaur skeleton climbing structures.

Connor climbed the skeleton of a dinosaur tail. Ruby climbed the dinosaur's ribs. Nick lay in between the teeth of the dinosaur's head with his mouth wide open, pretending to scream. Violet and Jasmine leaned on a baby dinosaur egg that was almost as tall as they were. Others sat on the stone wall of the garden.

Dad stood in front of the crowd. "Paleo Park would've been forests and swamps 110 million years ago." He pointed to the plants in the garden. "Did you know that these are prehistoric plants?"

"Really?" Ruby asked.

"Yep," said Violet. Dad had already told her about the prehistoric plants here.

Pointing each out as he named them, Dad said, "These ginkgoes, evergreens, horsetails, and ferns were around when the dinosaurs roamed here."

"Cool!" Connor hugged the dinosaur's tail.

"These plants couldn't be *that* old." Nick always took everything literally.

"These exact plants weren't around then," said Violet, "just the same kind of plants."

"Gotcha," said Nick.

Ms. Daisy entered the garden with a stack of papers. "Attention, brilliant buzzing brains and families! We have another exciting opportunity for our club, thanks to Violet's parents, Dr. Chen and Dr. Chen." Mom stood next to Ms. Daisy.

OMG! thought Violet. *This is really happening.*

"As you already know"—Ms. Daisy pointed to Mom— "Dr. Chen is a paleontologist"—then Ms. Daisy pointed to Dad—"and the other Dr. Chen is a botanist. They both work at the natural history museum in Pittsburgh. Our club has a chance to be volunteers for the new dinosaur exhibit."

Violet was having the best day! First, she found a dinosaur femur with Nick. Then, a hatchling on her own. And now she would get to hang out with the club at the natural history museum. Only her favorite place ever!

Finger snaps filled the garden like the popping noises of cicadas in the summer. The club always snapped to celebrate. Clapping was too loud for some of them. Cicadas wouldn't be at Paleo Park in December. But Dr. Hart had said they could find fossils of these prehistoric, red-eyed flying insects here. They were around when the dinosaurs lived.

Ms. Daisy passed around the permission slips. "On Monday after school, we'll be going to the natural history museum. We'll meet outside at the big dinosaur statue nicknamed Dippy. Anyone who wants to volunteer at the museum will need a permission slip from your parents."

"Why didn't you tell us?" Jasmine typed into her tablet. She always used it to communicate. Jasmine held up her tablet for Violet to read.

"I didn't know for sure," said Violet.

Violet smiled at Mom and Dad. They smiled back at Violet. It had been Violet's idea to have the Infinity Rainbow Club help with the new dinosaur exhibit. Mom had said she would talk to Ms. Daisy about it. But Mom didn't tell Violet that Ms. Daisy had said yes. *It will be the best club activity ever*, thought Violet. *And the best dinosaur exhibit too.*

But Violet worried that the exhibit wouldn't be ready for opening night. Or that something would go wrong at the museum. She would try not to check everything seven times. Mom and Dad wouldn't like that. But she wanted opening night to be amazing. And she would do whatever she had to do to make it perfect.

CHAPTER 3

On Sunday morning, Violet crawled out of bed and slid her tablet and field notebook into her backpack. She snuck downstairs before anyone else in her family was awake. Except for Lao Lao.

In the kitchen, Lao Lao diced up mango on a cutting board. The black tapioca pearls called boba sat in a container on the counter.

Mango boba! thought Violet. It was her favorite drink, made from fresh mango, mango juice, milk, ice, and boba.

"Good morning," said Lao Lao.

Violet raced over to the fridge and grabbed a full gallon of milk from it. "Good morning." She always made boba with Lao Lao on Sundays. But this Sunday was different. Violet had so many dinosaurs to check on the augmented reality app for the dinosaur exhibit. She needed to get started right away.

Violet tore off the plastic lid and tipped the container just enough to spill milk on the counter.

Lao Lao wiped up the milk. "Why the hurry?"

"I have to test the dinosaurs," said Violet. "Each one needs to be checked—" She was about to say seven times, but Lao Lao would say that two or three times is enough. Violet raced back to the fridge to grab the mango juice. "And I don't know if I'm going to run out of time"—she set the juice down on the counter—"and the exhibit needs to be perfect for opening night, and . . ." Violet blew air out of her mouth, hard. It was like she was trying to catch her breath after running in a race.

Lao Lao put her hand on Violet's shoulder. "I know the exhibit is going to be great. Checking the dinosaurs on the app is important. But taking care of yourself is too."

Lao Lao took a deep breath in. Violet did too and counted to seven in her head. They blew a deep breath out together. Violet counted to seven again. Lao Lao was the one who had taught her to take deep breaths like this. But not to count to seven—that was something Violet had added to the ritual. The breaths helped her calm her mind and body.

"So how about if we finish making mango boba?" said Lao Lao. "A little slower this time."

Violet smiled. She scooped out some boba with a spoon and plopped it into two reusable plastic cups. Then Violet dumped the mango cubes into the blender. Lao Lao poured the juice and milk in and Violet added the ice cubes.

After all the ingredients mixed together, Lao Lao poured the thick orange drink over boba in the plastic cups. Violet put lids on the cups and pushed wide straws into the holes on the lids. She took a sip and sucked up a boba pearl. Lao Lao did the same. The mango drink was sweet and the boba chewy. "Perfect," said Violet. Lao Lao nodded.

Violet put on her lavender winter coat and a matching set of white gloves, a hat, and a scarf. She flung her backpack over her shoulder.

"Take this." Lao Lao handed Violet an apple. Violet put it in her backpack. She grabbed her mango boba. Quietly opening the back door, she escaped into the yard just as the sun rose. It was Bo who she didn't want to wake up. The last thing she needed was him bothering her. She had work to do.

Violet rubbed the baby *T. rex* tooth on her neck back and forth seven times for good luck. She climbed the winding steps into the tree house.

In the woods, the pines and the spruces kept their needles. The brown leaves from the maple and oak trees covered the ground. The tree branches rustled in the wind. *Hoo-h'HOO-hoo-hoo*, called the great horned owl. *What a strange name for this owl*, thought Violet. *It doesn't have any horns, only two tufts of feathers on top of its head.* Its yellow eyes peered down from the nest high up in one of the pine trees.

Violet opened the museum app on her tablet. She clicked the augmented reality symbol at the bottom. It looked like a tablet with an eye on top of it. Boxes with images of different dinosaurs appeared on the screen. She chose the box for *Apatosaurus louisae*. A message flashed on the screen, "Move tablet to start."

Violet slowly moved the tablet in front of the window. Above and below the screen, the woods looked like they always did. On the screen, the same woods were there. But there was one *big* difference. A huge dinosaur stomped toward Violet on four legs that were as wide as tree trunks.

Apatosaurus louisae was one of the largest land mammals of all time. It was as tall as two school buses parked end to end. Some of the pine trees in Violet's backyard still towered over the dinosaur. They were as tall as three school buses.

On the tablet screen, the dinosaur moved toward her. Violet knew *Apatosaurus louisae* wasn't real. But seeing the dinosaur move through the trees in her backyard made it feel like it was really there.

The herbivore bent down its long neck. It chomped on pine needles and cones from a branch right next to the tree house window. *Evergreens are as old as dinosaurs*, thought Violet. *Of course it would eat pine needles and cones. But it wouldn't chew them like that*.

All that munching was making her hungry. Violet took a bite out of her apple. She slurped up her mango boba until she got another boba pearl.

When the dinosaur's head filled the screen, Violet jerked her head backward in surprise. *Does Apatosaurus louisae know I'm here?* she thought. She knew the question was silly. It wasn't a real dinosaur, after all. But its yellow eyes were looking right at her.

Violet slowly moved her head closer to the tablet. She put her hand outside the tree house window behind the tablet while looking at the screen. The palm of her hand was on the head of *Apatosaurus*. Violet knew she wasn't really touching its bluish-gray, leathery skin. But seeing her hand on the dinosaur's head made her feel like she was rubbing smooth, flat scales.

Violet closed the museum app. She put her tablet on the wooden desk built into the tree house wall. At the desk, Violet opened her field notebook to the section for the Jurassic Land exhibit.

She scanned her favorite list of seven, which she had written a few months ago. The exhibit had eight Jurassic dinosaurs. But Violet could *not* have a list of eight in her field notebook, so she had put the ornithopods in one item to make it a list of seven.

September 1
Natural History Museum
Dinosaurs for the Jurassic Land Exhibit

1. Camarasaurus lentus (sauropod, herbivore)
2. Ceratosaurus nasicornis (theropod, carnivore)
3. Dryosaurus altus (ornithopod, herbivore)
   Camptosaurus aphanoecetes (ornithopod, herbivore)
4. Apatosaurus louisae (sauropod, herbivore)
5. Stegosaurus armatus (stegosaur, herbivore)
6. Allosaurus fragilis (theropod, carnivore)
7. Diplodocus carnegii (sauropod, herbivore)

Violet flipped past the pages and pages of research she had done on these dinosaurs. Then Violet started a new entry:

December 9
Tree House
Augmented Reality Test #4
Apatosaurus louisae

Violet sketched the dinosaur. The body shape wasn't quite right. She grabbed her Stegosaurus eraser. She made another attempt. Still not quite right. It took her seven tries to get *Apatosaurus louisae* just right. The thick, elephant-like legs. The gray-blue, leathery skin. The whiplike tail. The curvy neck. The small head with nostrils on top of it. And the chisel-like teeth.

Under the drawing of *Apatosaurus louisae*, she made a list of seven:

1. Keep the dinosaur height, length, body shape, and color
2. Keep the dinosaur speed and stomping noises
3. Remove the dinosaur chewing pine needles and cones
4. Add the dinosaur using teeth to remove pine needles and cones from trees
5. Add the dinosaur swallowing pine needles and whole cones
6. Add the dinosaur swallowing stones to help grind the pine needles and cones
7. Move the dinosaur's neck down lower to balance with its tail

She checked off *Apatosaurus louisae* from her list of seven. *Only three more dinosaurs to go*, she thought. *The augmented reality for the exhibit is going to be amazing!*

Violet heard noise outside the tree house. *Thump. Thump. Thump.* The vibrations of the mango boba in her cup meant trouble. *Oh, no!* thought Violet. *Not now!*

CHAPTER 4

The thumps were getting louder and louder. And that meant closer and closer. They were right outside the tree house door. It flung open.

"You have to see this!" yelled Bo.

Violet knew he would wake up early. But she had hoped he would sleep in longer than this.

"No, I'm busy," Violet said.

"Why do you get mango boba?" asked Bo. "Can I try some?"

Violet took a sip of her boba. "You know Mom would say no. You'll choke on a boba pearl."

"No, I won't," said Bo. "What are you doing up here anyway?"

"I have to look at some dinosaurs," said Violet.

"You mean *those* dinosaurs?" Bo pointed up at the great horned owl nest. And then at the cardinals and blue jays on nearby trees. "But they're here every morning."

Ever since Bo learned that birds came from dinosaurs, he liked to call all the birds in their yard dinosaurs instead. He wasn't wrong. Feathered theropods eventually became birds. But Violet didn't have time for this. She needed to test out the other dinosaurs on the museum app on her tablet. She wanted to be ready when the club went to the natural history museum tomorrow after school.

Bo tapped a thick stick almost as tall as he was on the tree house floor. "But I want to show you my new secret hideout in . . ."

"I don't have time to bang sticks together with you!" Violet wanted to take the words back as soon as she said them. She wasn't trying to be mean.

Bo furrowed his eyebrows and crossed his arms. Violet used to battle Bo with sticks. But she was too old for that now. She wanted Bo to just leave her alone. "I'm working on augmented reality for the museum exhibit."

"Augminted what?" asked Bo.

The big words don't scare him off, thought Violet. "Augmented reality." Violet wished she hadn't told him what she was working on. He would want to know all about it now.

"What's that?" asked Bo.

"It's too hard to explain," said Violet.

"Please tell me." Bo widened his eyes and frowned. Mom called this his puppy-dog-eyes look.

"Okay, fine," said Violet. "I'll show you. But then you have to leave me alone."

"I'm ready." Bo put his stick down.

"Look out the window at the woods over there," said Violet. "Now, close your eyes." She propped her tablet up on the tree house window in front of Bo. She opened the museum app and selected a dinosaur. "Open your eyes."

About as tall as the tree house, *Stegosaurus armatus* stood among the trees. Its head was tiny in comparison to the rest of its thick neck and body. The brown skeletons of maple and oak trees glowed in the sun around the dinosaur. It had two rows of pentagon-shaped plates on its back. They looked like kites that changed from green to red.

The green skin of *Stegosaurus armatus* looked like it had honeycomb-shaped scales. Trudging along toward Violet and Bo, the dinosaur dragged its tail with spikes in it. *The tail looks perfect*, thought Violet. *But it shouldn't be dragging like that.*

"Whoa!" said Bo. "Look at that armor! The plates were for protection, right?"

"Maybe," said Violet. "Paleontologists don't know for sure. The plates might have changed to red as a warning sign. *Stegosaurus armatus* probably used the spikes on its tail to defend itself."

"He's a plant-eater, right?" asked Bo.

"Yep," said Violet. "*Stegosaurus armatus* is extinct, of course, but the app on my tablet makes it look like a real dinosaur is in our woods. It even moves like *Stegosaurus armatus*. Except for the tail that shouldn't be dragging. If you didn't already know it was extinct, you might think the dinosaur was real."

"So, this is augminted—I mean augmented—reality?" asked Bo.

"Yes." Violet moved the tablet from the window ledge. "Okay, the show is over. I have to get back to work."

"Wait!" said Bo. "Can I help you?"

"No." Violet sat down at her desk and opened her field notebook. On a new page, she created a new entry:

December 9
Tree House
Augmented Reality Test #5
Stegosaurus armatus

Violet started to sketch the dinosaur. Bo was still there. But she thought he would get bored watching her draw and leave.

"I have a cool idea for augmented reality," said Bo.

"Not now," said Violet.

Bo pointed to her field notebook. "What if you put—"

"Just leave me alone!" Violet yelled.

Bo snatched his stick and stomped out of the tree house. He slammed the door behind him. It sounded like he was banging his stick on each step of the winding stairs. Then the banging stopped. Violet looked up from her field notebook toward the window, but she couldn't see Bo. *Thud, thud, thud*, Violet heard.

In her imagination, Bo slid down the tree house stairs and hit his head. Blood ran down his face from a gash above his eyebrow too.

More unwanted thoughts. Violet didn't want any of the horrible things she imagined to happen. But she didn't have control over them either.

Violet jumped up and ran to the tree house door. She jerked it open and peered down the stairs. Bo was on his feet at the bottom. She couldn't see any blood.

"Are you okay?" asked Violet.

"Yeah. Did you have another one of your unwanted thoughts?" asked Bo.

Violet nodded her head.

Bo waved his stick in the air. "Look, I'm totally fine. Promise."

"Okay, I believe you." Violet remembered the day she told Bo about her OCD. It was in the tree house on a hot day last summer. She told him about the time she imagined Lao Lao starting a kitchen fire that burned the house down with their whole family in it. And Mom falling off a cliff on a digging expedition. And Dad getting eaten by a jaguar in the Amazon.

At first, Bo thought she was joking. And Violet was sorry she had told him about her intrusive thoughts. But then he asked more questions. Violet told him about her lists of seven and how she checked everything seven times. He said that he had seen her doing those things. And after that, he understood.

There was no end to Violet's horrible thoughts. Every day was a fight for her to gain control. But right now, Bo was safe. He ran through the woods, using his stick to bat away low-hanging branches. She went back in the tree house and continued to test the dinosaurs.

CHAPTER 5

Violet sat up on her bed. A mural of Jurassic dinosaurs surrounded her on the walls. Her mural had some of the same dinosaurs as the one around the Jurassic Land exhibit. But hers wasn't nearly as big.

On the wall behind her bed, she used a finger to outline two green *Stegosauri armatus.* Their red plates and tails with spikes paraded through a bed of ferns. She next traced the sauropods. *Apatosaurus* and *Diplodocus* towered over her dresser with their elephant-like bodies and tree-trunk-sized legs poking out. Their long necks balanced their long tails.

And then there were the theropods. Near one corner of the room, she outlined a meat-eating *Ceratosaurus nasicornis* walking on two legs. It had a large head, horns on its snout and above its eyes, steak-knife teeth, and short arms with four claws on each hand. On the wall surrounding the door, she traced two *Allosauri fragilis* that were even bigger meat-eating dinosaurs. They walked on two legs and had large heads, steak-knife teeth, and three claws on each hand.

Tracing the seven dinosaurs on her mural helped Violet calm her body and mind. She always did them in the same order. First stegosaurs, next sauropods, and then theropods.

Violet moved on to tracing the plants painted on the wall. She outlined the tree fern with large fronds, or leaves, sticking out of what looked like a large trunk. Dad had explained that the trunk was actually roots. He also said the tree fern was a fern but not a tree.

Violet traced the horsetail stems with cone-shaped tips. They were hollow and reminded her of bamboo stalks. She

had to have horsetails in her room. They were truly ancient. Horsetails have been around for at least 300 million years!

Violet remembered that she hadn't watered the real plants today. And even worse, she couldn't remember the last time she watered them. Yesterday, they were at Paleo Park all day. She forgot to water them before they left for the park. It must've been Friday then. *Oh no!* thought Violet. She imagined the plants shriveled up and brown.

Violet took a deep breath in, counting to seven. She let out a deep breath, counting to seven again. The plants weren't dead. They were totally fine in the corners of her room. Still as green as ever.

Violet grabbed her watering can and headed to the bathroom sink. It hadn't been hard to convince Dad to get prehistoric plants for her bedroom. Even the same ones that were part of the dinosaur exhibit. After all, Dad was a botanist with his own greenhouse in the backyard. Dad couldn't say no to plants.

Mom didn't think Violet needed plants in her bedroom because they had a greenhouse. But she let Violet have potted horsetails and a tree fern if she promised to water them. Violet tried really hard to remember. But she usually forgot to water the plants for more days than she remembered to. The tree fern was already as tall as Violet. Another reason Mom didn't think she needed plants in her room.

Violet had filled the watering can halfway when she heard Lao Lao call from the kitchen, "Violet!" Even from the upstairs bathroom, Violet could smell the spicy beef noodle soup that Lao Lao had spent all day simmering. *Not again*, she had thought when she saw Lao Lao chopping beef after her morning walk.

"Dinner!" Lao Lao yelled up the stairs.

"Be right there!" Violet watered her plants before going downstairs.

The family gathered around the table for Sunday dinner. Mom and Dad would have to work a lot of late nights at the museum to get ready for opening night on Friday. This would be the only night this week that the whole family ate dinner together at their house.

Beef noodle soup was Lao Lao's favorite dish to make. She had told Violet that it was a secret family recipe carried down for three generations before her.

Beef noodle soup used to be Violet's favorite meal. But one time she got sick from the soup. The whole family got sick. Bad beef, Mom had said when it happened a few years ago. But no one seemed to remember the bad beef except for Violet.

Now every time she smelled stewed beef, Violet still felt a little sick to her stomach. But Lao Lao went through a lot of trouble making beef noodle soup. And she really enjoyed making it too. How could Violet say anything bad about it?

At the dinner table, steam rose from the bowls with a shiny film of spicy chili oil floating on top of the broth. Violet stared at the noodles piled high in her bowl with beef chunks swimming in the broth. Using chopsticks, Dad lifted noodles into the broth on his soup spoon.

What if Lao Lao didn't cook the beef the right way? Violet thought. She knew the beef had been cooked most of the day, but that wasn't enough to convince her to eat it. She imagined taking a bite of beef and throwing up. *Eating seven noodles and then one beef chunk will make it safe*, thought Violet. *But Mom and Dad won't like it if they see me eating this way*.

Bo dug into his bowl with chopsticks and splashed drops of soup on the table. He was always the messiest eater. Bo reminded Violet of a dinosaur eating with the loud *chomp*, *chomp*, *chomp* noise he made with the beef chunks.

Mom drank the broth with a soup spoon. She turned toward Lao Lao. "Excellent as always, Mom."

"You really outdid yourself with this batch," said Dad.

Lao Lao smiled.

"Mmmm." Bo licked his lips.

Violet was the only one who hadn't tasted the soup yet. She used her chopsticks to gather two long noodles on her soup spoon. She slurped each noodle to the end and turned to Lao Lao. "Very good." Violet fished for two more noodles. And two more. Then, one more noodle to get to a total of seven noodles. Out of the corner of her eye, she saw Dad watching her, but he didn't say anything.

Violet turned toward Mom. "I tested the Jurassic dinosaurs on the app this morning."

"Violet showed me *Stegosaurus armorus*," Bo said.

"*Stegosaurus ar-MA-TUS*," Violet corrected him.

"But she wouldn't let me see the rest." Bo put down his chopsticks and turned to Violet with his pouty face.

"Don't worry, Bo," said Dad. "You'll get a chance to see all the dinosaurs. Violet was helping Mom get them ready for opening night."

"Which dinosaurs did you test?" Mom wiped her mouth with a napkin.

"The rest of them." Violet counted the beef pieces floating in her bowl. There were six, so she used her chopstick to break one chunk into two. *Seven beef chunks will be less likely to make me sick*, Violet thought.

She took a deep breath in and counted to seven. Then she let it out, counting to seven again. Her chopsticks shook as she lifted the first beef chunk to her mouth. She chewed it very slowly.

"Wow, that was fast!" Mom loaded her chopsticks with a mouthful of noodles. "Did the tech team do a good job with them?"

"They're mostly good, but I have some changes." Violet didn't feel sick after eating the first piece of beef. But she decided to eat seven more noodles before the next beef chunk just in case.

Dad whispered in her ear. "I know you're counting seven noodles and beef chunks." He knew Violet wouldn't want anyone else to hear him correcting her.

Violet didn't argue and waited for him to finish.

"Nothing bad will happen if you don't count them," he whispered. "Could you try to eat your food without counting it?"

Violet nodded. She knew he was right. And she would try to make it through dinner without counting any more food. But sometimes it was really hard not to.

Mom dipped her soup spoon into her bowl to fill it with beef broth. "You're saving me and the other scientists a lot of time by catching mistakes. The dinosaurs will be much more realistic too." Mom knew Dad had corrected Violet. But Mom pretended nothing had happened. She knew it would be embarrassing for Violet to have everyone at the dinner table talk about her OCD.

"And don't forget about the plants." Dad smiled.

"What about the plants?" asked Violet. "Did you add *more* of them to the magic mirror library?"

"Maaaaybe." Dad always stretched out *maybe* like that was the right way to say it. "You'll see."

"I knew you would," said Violet. *Maybe* always meant "yes" to Dad.

"What's a magic mirror?" asked Bo.

"It's a big screen on the wall of an empty room in the museum," said Mom. "When you look at the screen, you see yourself standing next to dinosaurs."

"I can't wait to see the magic mirror tomorrow!" said Bo.

"But you're not volunteering at the museum, Bo," said Violet. "I'm going with my club to help get the museum ready for opening night."

"Lao Lao is taking me too," said Bo.

Violet shot a look at Lao Lao, who nodded her head.

"But Bo will get in the way," said Violet. He wouldn't leave her alone. Violet had to focus on the augmented reality exhibit. Not on answering Bo's endless questions.

"Don't talk about your brother like that," said Dad.

"Connor's brother, Luke, is in the club," said Mom. "And he's in Bo's first-grade class. Luke's mom said he's coming."

"A lot of young kids come to the museum, Violet," said Lao Lao. "Remember that you were one of them. *Dinosaur* was one of your first words. But you called it 'duna.'"

Bo laughed. "Me too!"

"I know the story." Violet smiled. "You've only told us a hundred times."

Lao Lao always said that Violet had loved dinosaurs since she was a baby. Violet stopped crying when she saw dinosaur bones from her stroller. She crawled around on the museum floor before she could walk. And Violet pointed at dinosaur skeletons and yelled, "Duna!"

Violet and Lao Lao would stare at the lovely bones and memorize all their bumps and grooves. That never changed over the years. When he could crawl, Violet taught Bo how to say "duna" too.

"I bet Bo will come up with great ideas for the augmented reality exhibit." Lao Lao winked at Bo.

"Fine," said Violet. "But he's not staying with me."

CHAPTER 6

After school on Monday, Lao Lao drove Violet, Nick, Grace, and Bo to the natural history museum. The club met outside. Infinity Rainbow Club T-shirts poked out of their coats.

The dinosaur statue of *Diplodocus carnegii* towered over them. It was the museum's mascot, nicknamed Dippy. Like other sauropods, he had a small head, an elephant-like body, tree-trunk-sized legs, and a long tail. The shrubs circling Dippy made the space feel like a small garden.

Nick had been to the museum enough times to know about Dippy. But Connor, Ruby, and Jasmine had never been to the museum before. Violet couldn't wait until they saw the dinosaurs for the first time.

Jasmine took photos of the Dippy statue. Nick told Connor and Ruby about the scarves and hats that Dippy always wore. Thanks to Dad, it was a black and gold football scarf this time. Connor's little brother, Luke, and Bo banged sticks together.

Flipping through her field notebook, Violet read her entries about the augmented reality exhibit. She was ready!

"Brilliant buzzing brains!" said Ms. Daisy. Under her coat, Ms. Daisy wore her Infinity Rainbow Club T-shirt too. She pointed at the statue. "This is one of the most famous dinosaurs in the world."

"Really?" Jasmine wrote on her tablet. She showed her tablet to Violet. Violet nodded.

"What about *T. rex*?" asked Connor.

"*T. rex* is very famous too," said Ms. Daisy. "We'll learn more about the story behind Dippy inside the museum. Okay, we're all here," said Ms. Daisy. "Follow me!"

The club entered the museum and walked by the large windows in front of the fossil lab. A man with long white hair and a matching beard was working inside.

"It's Dr. Hart!" said Violet.

The club peered into the windows. Dr. Hart looked up at them and smiled. This time Violet knew it was a smile buried under his beard. He came out of the lab.

"What are you doing here?" asked Violet.

"I'm helping out in the fossil lab," said Dr. Hart.

"I thought you only worked in the Washington, DC, natural history museum," said Nick.

"Yeah, I've never seen you here before," said Violet. "What are you working on?"

"A large dinosaur femur from the Cretaceous period," said Dr. Hart.

"Like the *Astrodon johnstoni* Nick and I found?" asked Violet.

"C'mon," Dr. Hart said. "Let me show you and Nick." He turned to Ms. Daisy. "The rest of the kids can have a turn in the lab later."

Ms. Daisy nodded. The fossil lab wasn't big enough for the whole group to go in at the same time. Violet and Nick entered the lab with Dr. Hart. The rest of the club watched through the windows with Ms. Daisy.

Field jackets lay on the lab bench.

"Where did these come from?" asked Violet. "They look just like—"

"—our field jackets," Nick chimed in, pointing to the date marked on the outside of them.

"They *are* the fossils we found at Paleo Park!" said Violet.

Nick flapped his hands. Violet wanted to jump up and down. But she didn't want to break anything in the lab.

"But how?" asked Nick.

"All the fossils the club and their families found at Paleo Park are here," said Dr. Hart. "They're on loan from the museum in Washington, DC."

Mom and Dad entered the lab. Mom wore a green T-shirt with a gold Dippy on it. And Dad had a black T-shirt with a gold Dippy.

"Why didn't you tell me?" Violet hugged Mom and Dad.

"It was a surprise," said Dad.

"But it wasn't our idea." Mom turned toward Dr. Hart.

"I thought we could show everyone how fossils get ready for museum display," said Dr. Hart. "Do you want to work with me in the fossil lab on opening night?"

"You mean, we get to clean the fossils?" asked Violet.

Dr. Hart nodded.

"No way!" said Nick.

"I'm in!" said Violet.

"Me too!" said Nick.

Violet loved cleaning fossils. But it was hard work. After the dig in Wyoming last summer, she brought back fossils to the natural history museum. She spent months cleaning them with Mom's help. They were so fragile.

The fossils from Paleo Park would be easy to break too. After all, they were 110 million years old. The clay was the only thing keeping them together. There was no room for mistakes. *What if we break the fossils while trying to clean them?* thought Violet. *And in front of a crowd on opening night?*

In her imagination, the femur bone cracked down the middle like an earthquake had hit it. And the hatchling bones crumbled on the lab bench. But Violet knew that these were intrusive thoughts.

The fossils were safe in their field jackets. And Dr. Hart would make sure they cleaned them the right way. Opening night was going to be perfect. She was sure of it. No unwanted or bad thoughts were going to change that.

CHAPTER 7

In the natural history museum, the grayish, brownish, and reddish-brown dinosaur bones towered over the club. Over millions of years, the fossils had changed. They slowly became the color of the minerals in the ground where they were found.

"This is the Jurassic Atrium!" said Ms. Daisy.

Violet spun in a circle to take it all in. She was just as excited as the rest of the club. It didn't matter that she had been here too many times to count. The old bones of creatures that no longer lived made her feel more alive than anything else.

Over the years, the way the bones were put together changed. Some dinosaurs were added. And some were taken apart and put back together a different way. The paleontologists had learned more about how the dinosaurs looked, moved, and lived. Mom said *Apatosaurus louisae* had the wrong head for forty-five years. And Lao Lao said she remembered when the natural history museum changed the skull to the right one.

The dinosaur skeletons looked like they stood next to real trees and plants. The browns of trunks and the bright green patches of vegetation in the exhibit were artificial. But Dad had spent years doing research to get the Jurassic trees and plants just right for the museum. The ferns, cycads, horsetails, cypresses, pines, araucarias, and ginkgoes were around when these dinosaurs lived.

The museum mural on the walls around the Jurassic Atrium was one of the largest in the world. It stood as tall as a streetlight and stretched longer than the fifty-yard dash. Wrapping around the room, the mural blended in with the bones on display. *It doesn't feel like a closed room*, thought Violet. The dinosaurs parading around the landscape kept going and going off into the distance.

"Let's head over to Dippy!" said Ms. Daisy.

The club walked toward the center of the Jurassic Atrium. *Diplodocus carnegii* and *Apatosaurus louisae* stretched and stretched across it. Walking around them on all sides was the only way to see their huge skeletons.

The club stretched their necks up as high as they could go. Their mouths dropped open. The sauropod dinosaurs were mighty and strong. But there wasn't a word to describe how amazing they were. Their small heads on their long necks were turned toward each other. It looked like they could be communicating.

Dinosaur bones were a window into the past. Violet felt like she had traveled in a time machine. That she had stepped into another world, where dinosaurs ruled. *Maybe someday a time machine will be invented to go back to the time of the dinosaurs*, thought Violet.

"How many of the dinosaur bones are real?" Ruby asked Violet.

"About 75 percent of them," said Violet.

"Whoa," said Ruby. "That's a lot."

The club gathered next to Dippy. He had a long and skinny skeleton, about the length of two school buses. *Diplodocus carnegii* had thinner bones than *Apatosaurus louisae.* Like a giraffe, Dippy had a long neck that bent easily. But a giraffe had seven long neck bones. Dippy had fifteen or more of them that fit together like a puzzle.

"Brilliant buzzing brains!" said Ms. Daisy. "We will be testing the augmented reality using tablets around the museum. You can use the museum tablets at the docking stations in front of each dinosaur that's part of the Jurassic Land exhibit." Ms. Daisy picked up one of the museum tablets in front of Dippy. "The easiest way to see a dinosaur with augmented reality is to scan the

QR code next to the dinosaur display. You can use the museum tablets or your own for this. Sharing tablets is a good idea too. The museum also has an app that you can download on your tablet to see the augmented reality dinosaurs in the museum or even at home."

Violet, Nick, and Jasmine had their own tablets. Some other club members had brought their own too.

"Violet, are you ready to show the club how the augmented reality works?" asked Ms. Daisy.

"Sure," said Violet. "You scan the QR code like this." She held her tablet screen in front of the funny-looking box with black and white squares. "Then you can move the tablet so it's pointed at Dippy's skeleton. And the bones come to life with flesh and reddish-brown skin. Dippy stands right in front of you on the tablet. And everything else in the atrium is still on the screen too."

On the tablet, Dippy stomped along with his whiplike tail swinging back and forth. Narrow, pointy spikes ran all the way down his back and tail. They looked like spikes on an iguana.

"You can watch it eat too." Violet pushed a button on the tablet.

Dippy reached down with his peg-like teeth. He broke off fern leaves and swallowed them whole.

"Sauropods didn't chew their food," said Violet.

Dippy picked up stones with his teeth.

On her tablet, Jasmine typed, "He ate stones?" The voice on her tablet said the words out loud.

"Yep, he swallowed stones to help digest the leaves." Violet remembered the augmented reality tests she had done in the tree house. Having the sauropods swallow whole leaves and stones had been on her list of changes for them. *Diplodocus carnegii looks much more realistic now*, Violet thought.

"You can zoom in like this." Violet put her index finger and thumb on the tablet screen and spread them apart. "And you can move the tablet like this"—she rotated her tablet around to different angles—"to view the dinosaur from above or in front."

Mom had joined the group and was smiling at Violet.

"Perfect timing," said Ms. Daisy to Mom. Ms. Daisy turned toward the club. "You remember Violet's mom, Dr. Chen, from Paleo Park. She's going to tell us more about Dippy. You can look at him on the tablets while listening. It will be the same story she's going to tell on opening night. We're going to let Dr. Chen practice with us."

"Who wants to know why Dippy is so famous?" asked Mom.

The club answered with a chorus of "I do, I do!"

Bo was always the loudest. And he already knew the Dippy story by heart, just like Violet. She used to beg Mom to tell her the Dippy story over and over again. It was one of her favorite stories about the dinosaurs.

It was Violet's idea for Mom to tell this story to introduce Dippy on opening night for the new exhibit. *Will the club like the story as much as I do?* wondered Violet. *What about the people I don't know who will be coming on opening night?*

CHAPTER 8

The kids in the club shared tablets with *Diplodocus carnegii* stomping all over the Jurassic Atrium. They were more than ready to hear the story behind Dippy.

"'Most Colossal Animal Ever on Earth Just Found Out West,'" said Mom. "Andrew Carnegie, the founder of the natural history museum, read this newspaper headline in 1898."

"Whoa!" Connor backed away from Nick's tablet. The reddish-brown scaly skin on Dippy's head filled the screen. The head looked a lot bigger zoomed in like that.

"And there's more," said Mom. "The article said that when it ate, the dinosaur filled a stomach large enough to hold three elephants."

"What!" Bo always said this when he heard about its huge stomach.

"And when it was angry, the dinosaur's terrible roar could be heard for ten miles," said Mom.

"No way!" Nick said.

Violet pulled out her field notebook. But she didn't

start a new entry. She turned to a list she had made a few months ago. A list she made with Mom to help her prepare for the Dippy story. Violet read the entry to check the details:

September 15
Natural History Museum
Diplodocus carnegii (Dippy)

1. Andrew Carnegie read 1898 newspaper headline: "Most Colossal Animal Ever on Earth Just Found Out West."

"Carnegie *really* wanted to buy the dinosaur for Pittsburgh," said Mom. "But when a team of paleontologists went out West to dig it up, it wasn't there. The newspaper headline about the huge dinosaur was mostly made up."

On the tablet screen, Dippy swung his whiplike tail toward Violet. She backed away from it. She knew his tail wasn't actually going to hit her. But in the moment, it felt like it could. *That's what he would do to defend himself*, she thought.

"A piece of a large leg bone was found," said Mom, "but nowhere near a whole dinosaur."

"How could the newspaper make all of that up?"

asked Ruby. She craned her neck to follow Jasmine's tablet screen high in the air. They looked under Dippy's stomach.

Violet hoped they weren't checking to see if it could fit three elephants.

"They shouldn't have made it up," said Mom. "It certainly wasn't good newspaper reporting."

Violet looked at her field notebook entry:

2. Carnegie wanted to buy the colossal dinosaur for Pittsburgh.

3. A team of paleontologists went out West to dig up the dinosaur.

4. But the story in the newspaper was made up. Only part of a femur had been found. Not a huge dinosaur.

"So, then what happened?" asked Matt.

"The team of paleontologists that went out West found a really big dinosaur in 1899," said Mom. "Carnegie got his colossal dinosaur after all. The team sent back 130 crates full of fossils that filled an entire boxcar on a train! And guess what kind of dinosaur was in those crates?"

"Dippy!" the group called out together. Violet knew it

had to be her imagination. But she felt like Dippy stared back at her through the tablet screen. It was like the dinosaur knew he was being called by name. Bo and Luke pointed at Dippy on Violet's screen.

"That's right," said Mom. "They cleaned the bones and knew it was a new species of dinosaur. It was named *Diplodocus carnegii* after Andrew Carnegie. A year later, they found another *Diplodocus carnegii*."

"Awesome!" said Nick's sister Grace.

"What you see here"—Mom pointed to the Dippy skeleton—"is 90 percent original. All the bones from the first *Diplodocus carnegii* are here. And the bones that were missing from the first dinosaur came from the second one. About 10 percent of the bones are plaster casts."

Any bones of *Diplodocus carnegii* that the museum had two copies of were stored in the secret Big Bone Room. Violet had seen them when Mom took her in it. Mom said the Big Bone Room was like a library of dinosaur bones.

Violet read the next entry in her field notebook:

5. In 1899, the Carnegie team dug up Diplodocus carnegii. A year later they found another one. Dippy is 90% original fossil.

Violet listened to the story like it was the first time she had heard it. She knew even more details from Mom. Back then, paleontologists raced to be the first to discover new dinosaurs. They found thousands of dinosaur bones. But they fought over them and even damaged each other's fossil finds. Mom said it was called the Bone Wars. Violet was glad Mom wasn't around for that.

"Carnegie sent casts of the 85-foot-long dinosaur to cities around the world," said Mom. "A lot of these museums still have copies of Dippy on display. And that's how he got to be so famous. But the real bones are right here in this museum." Mom pointed at them.

"They're amazing!" said Jasmine's sister, Destiny.

Nick used his tablet to zoom into the spikes on Dippy's back. They looked like they could cause some real damage.

"In 1999, Dippy got a statue to celebrate his one-hundred-year anniversary," said Mom. "The one you saw outside before you came into the museum."

6. Carnegie sent 10 casts (copies) of Dippy around the world.

7. In 1999, Dippy got a statue for his 100-year anniversary.

"Thank you so much, Dr. Chen," said Ms. Daisy.

Everyone snapped.

They took turns in the fossil lab with Dr. Hart. And they wandered around the Jurassic Atrium testing the augmented reality dinosaurs on tablets. The exhibit included sauropods, theropods, ornithopods, and a stegosaur.

In her field notebook, Violet looked at her list of dinosaurs for the Jurassic Land exhibit:

September 1
Natural History Museum
Dinosaurs for the Jurassic Land Exhibit

1. Camarasaurus lentus (sauropod, herbivore)
2. Ceratosaurus nasicornis (theropod, carnivore)
3. Dryosaurus altus (ornithopod, herbivore)
   Camptosaurus aphanoecetes (ornithopod, herbivore)
4. Apatosaurus louisae (sauropod, herbivore)
5. Stegosaurus armatus (stegosaur, herbivore)
6. Allosaurus fragilis (theropod, carnivore)
7. Diplodocus carnegii (sauropod, herbivore)

Keeping track of the dinosaurs she tested helped Violet calm her body and mind. Each item needed to be checked seven times before opening night. The first set of check marks next to each item were from her tests at the tree house. She had spent the last hour in the museum working her way through the second round of tests. She had two check marks next to each item. Except for one. *Allosaurus fragilis.*

Violet, Jasmine, and Ruby huddled around Violet's tablet screen. Running toward them on two legs, *Allosaurus fragilis* was in attack mode. The cream-colored underbelly of this bluish-gray dinosaur bounced as it ran. Spines ran down its back from the neck to the tail. It came closer and closer. The yellow stripes across

its back blurred together. Three fingers on each hand ended in sharp claws ready to strike.

Ruby ducked below the tablet.

Jasmine looked down at her.

Ruby stood up again. "I'm not scared," she said to Jasmine. "You're scared."

Violet zoomed in on the large snout and flaring nostrils. Thin triangle-shaped orange horns sat in front of its eyes. *How can he see with those horns in the way?* Violet wondered.

Jasmine wrote on her tablet. "Uh, you're the one shaking," said the voice on her tablet. Jasmine smiled.

The steak-knife teeth of *Allosaurus fragilis* were opened wide. They were ready to tear off flesh. *Now that's how you made a predator*, thought Violet.

Violet looked toward Ruby. "You *are* shaking," Violet said to Ruby and laughed. "But you're safe for tonight." Violet shut down her tablet. She added the last check mark to the list in her field notebook. It was time to go.

There is so much left to do before opening night! thought Violet. *I can't be everywhere I need to be at the same time.* The dinosaurs that appeared in the magic mirror needed to be checked. The fossil lab needed to be set up the right way. And the augmented reality stations in front of the dinosaurs needed to be checked again too. Violet took a deep breath in, counting to seven. And a deep breath out, counting to seven.

"What are we going to do tomorrow?" asked Ruby.

"We're going to test the magic mirror," said Violet.

"What's that?" asked the voice on Jasmine's tablet.

"It's a big screen where you can see yourself surrounded by dinosaurs," said Violet. "You can interact with them too."

"What!" said Ruby. "I can't wait."

"This is going to be so much fun!" said the voice on Jasmine's tablet.

Jasmine is right, thought Violet. *Testing the magic mirror is going to be awesome.* Jurassic dinosaurs would come together in one place on one screen. And Violet would have the club here to help her.

All they had to do was make sure it was the best augmented reality dinosaur exhibit the world had ever seen. How hard could that be? It just had to be absolutely perfect. The showstopper for opening night. *No pressure at all*, thought Violet.

CHAPTER 9

On Tuesday, Violet stared at the grayish-white walls of her classroom. They reminded her of the sky right before a storm. A sky threatening to pour rain at any moment. And she wanted so badly to escape. Violet rubbed the baby *T. rex* tooth on her necklace seven times. She told herself that doing this would help her make it through the school day.

The grayish-white wall near her table had small grooves and bumps like the fossils she found at Paleo Park. She would much rather be there instead of at school. Or even better, at the natural history museum in rooms full of bones.

"All right class, it's time for science," said Ms. Wishbone. "We're going to be dinosaur detectives today!"

Dinosaur detectives! thought Violet. *Maybe science class won't be so bad after all.* She took her field notebook out of her backpack. Anything about dinosaurs *had* to be recorded in her field notebook. She opened it up to a blank page and started a new entry:

December 11
Deer Park Elementary School
Science Class
Dinosaur Detectives

"Does anyone know the history of the word *dinosaur*?" asked Ms. Wishbone. Her black rectangle glasses perched on the end of her nose looked like they were about to fall. Violet waited for Ms. Wishbone to push them back up her nose to read. She imagined them tumbling to the floor and cracking.

Nick and Ruby turned toward Violet. Then the rest of the class shifted in their seats to see Violet too. *Why are they staring at me?* she wondered. Violet could feel her face turning red. Of course she knew the answer to the question. No one ever asked a dinosaur question that Violet didn't know. She probably knew more about dinosaurs than Ms. Wishbone.

Violet kept her eyes on the whiteboard. Maybe if she pretended not to notice, the class would stop looking at her. But it didn't work.

Talking in front of the whole class terrified Violet. It wasn't the same as talking in front of the club. Her friends knew she was different. No one in the club would

make fun of her lists. Or think she was weird for checking everything seven times. But maybe the class would stop staring at her if she just answered the question. She raised her shaking hand. This was the first time she had volunteered to answer a question in front of the class.

Ms. Wishbone pointed at her. "Violet."

"Sir Richard . . . Owen. He . . . was . . . a . . ." Violet could feel the class staring at her even more than before. Why couldn't she get the words out? Violet wanted to get the answer just right. But she sounded like she didn't even know the answer.

Ms. Wishbone added the name to the whiteboard.

Violet took a deep breath in, counting to seven. And a deep breath out, counting to seven. "He was . . . a paleontologist," said Violet. "He came up with . . . the word *dinosaur* in 1842."

Ms. Wishbone added the year to the whiteboard.

"Whoa," said a boy named Liam, "That was a long time ago."

The class was still looking at Violet. But it felt different now. Like they were impressed with her answer. And they were waiting for her to tell them more.

"He combined two Greek words," said Violet. "*Deinos*

means terrible. And *sauros* means lizard. Dinosaur means 'terrible lizard.'"

"Wow!" someone behind her said. "I didn't know that."

"But I don't think they were terrible at all," said Violet. "Dinosaurs were amazing creatures."

"Excellent!" Ms. Wishbone added more notes to the whiteboard.

Violet copied the words into her field notebook:

1. Paleontologist Sir Richard Owen first used the word dinosaur in 1842.
2. Deinos (Greek) = Terrible (English)
3. Sauros (Greek) = Lizard (English)

Violet liked to keep a record of anything about dinosaurs. It didn't matter that she already knew these facts. Besides, those were her words on the whiteboard. Words that she had said in front of the whole class. Maybe she had turned red. Maybe it wasn't perfect. But it wasn't as bad as she'd thought it would be. It was the first time she talked in class and didn't hate it. She wished they would talk about dinosaurs at school again.

"Okay, let's try another question," said Ms. Wishbone.

"How long ago did the dinosaurs live? I'll give you a hint. It was millions of years ago."

Violet looked around the classroom to see if Nick or Ruby had raised their hand. They had learned this at the natural history museum.

Violet held her breath. *Answering one question is enough for today*, Violet thought.

Ruby put up her hand. Violet let out her breath. Ms. Wishbone called on Ruby.

"You mean the dinosaurs that didn't become birds?" asked Ruby.

Violet smiled. That was exactly what she was thinking.

Ms. Wishbone nodded her head.

"They lived between about 245 and 66 million years ago," said Ruby.

"Great!" Ms. Wishbone put the years on the whiteboard. Violet made a note of them in her field notebook. But she already knew the years.

"Here's another question," said Ms. Wishbone. "What are dinosaur tracks and trackways? It's okay to make an educated guess."

A girl named Sarah raised her hand. Ms. Wishbone called on her. "Dinosaur tracks are dinosaur footprints,"

Sarah said. "I think dinosaur trackways would be a path of dinosaur tracks. They would show where the dinosaurs had walked or run."

"Exactly right," said Ms. Wishbone. In her field notebook, Violet copied what Ms. Wishbone wrote on the whiteboard:

4. Track = Footprint
5. Trackway = Path
6. Trackways show where dinosaurs had walked or run.

"Does anyone know what they call a scientist who studies dinosaur tracks?" asked Ms. Wishbone.

Nick knows the answer, thought Violet. She had told him about her visit to a dinosaur track site in Wyoming last summer. Nick never forgot anything. He raised his hand. Ms. Wishbone called on him. "An ichnologist," Nick said.

In her field notebook, Violet copied the definition that Ms. Wishbone put on the whiteboard.

7. An ichnologist studies dinosaur tracks.

"Okay, that's it for class discussion," said Ms. Wishbone. "Now we're going to move into groups."

A perfect place to stop, thought Violet. Everything fit into one list of seven. Any more notes would've needed a new list.

"We're going to learn more about the amazing tracks that dinosaurs left behind," said Ms. Wishbone, "and what the tracks tell us about how dinosaurs lived. We have two science centers: dinosaur math and dinosaur trackways. The assigned groups for your centers are on the whiteboard. Please move to your centers."

First, Violet had dinosaur math with Ruby and Nick. Violet was good at math. *Really* good. But she thought Nick and Ruby were math geniuses. They always finished math problems before her. Did they even check their answers? Maybe she would be better at dinosaur math. At least, she knew more than they did about dinosaurs.

CHAPTER 10

For the dinosaur math center, Violet sat at a table with
Nick and Ruby. A boy named Owen joined their table too.
Cutouts of dinosaur tracks, rulers, and worksheets were
piled up on the table. Violet started a new entry in her
field notebook:

Center #1
Dinosaur Math

Owen read the instructions out loud. "Ichnologists measure the length of a dinosaur track from the heel to the tip of its center claw to estimate a dinosaur's height. Every inch of the track is equal to about one foot or twelve inches in height."

"Easy enough." Ruby tapped her perfectly sharpened pencil on the table.

Violet began another list of seven in her field notebook:

1. Measure dinosaur track from heel to toe
2. 1 inch length of dinosaur track = 12 inches height of dinosaur

"Are you good, Violet?" Nick popped the bubbles on his green *T. rex* fidget. He turned it over and popped them in the other direction.

"Yep." Violet was done writing in her notebook. But looking ahead at the worksheet, she noticed a problem. The worksheet had only four questions. She couldn't have a list of six. *How can this be a list of seven?* she wondered.

Violet read the first question out loud and copied it into her field notebook:

3. Find the baby dinosaur track labeled #1. Measure it from heel to toe. How tall is the baby dinosaur?

She measured the baby dinosaur track with a ruler. "Two inches." In her notebook, Violet wrote:

2 x 12 = 24 in.

"Are you ready?" Ruby tapped her pencil again. Violet hated it when she did that. What was the rush? Nick popped his fidget again. Of course, Ruby and Nick knew the answer right away. No special facts about dinosaurs were needed to answer the question. Owen was done before Violet too. But he took longer than Ruby and Nick.

"No, I need to check my answer." Violet did the math in her head seven times and got the same answer. She thought she had the right answer the first time. And she was sure she got the right answer the second time. But she had to do the math seven times just in case. "Done."

"I got twenty-four inches." Nick tore a small piece of paper out of his notebook and wrote on it.

"Me too," said Ruby.

"Me, three," said Violet.

Owen nodded.

They put the answer on their worksheets.

Nick folded up the piece of paper and handed it to Violet.

She read Nick's note: "I know you're checking your answers seven times." Violet had asked Nick to remind her when she was being compulsive. He wrote a note because he knew she would be embarrassed if he told her in front of the group.

Nick looked over at Violet. She nodded. But math problems were the hardest for her to resist sevens.

"Okay, I'll play the next question on my tablet." Ruby had a different brain like Violet. But Ruby was dyslexic. She needed extra help with reading.

Violet copied the question in her field notebook:

4. Find the dinosaur tracks labeled 2a and 2b. They're from two different dinosaurs. Measure the tracks from heel to toe. Which dinosaur is taller? By how much?

Owen measured the dinosaur track labeled 2a. "Five inches."

And Nick measured the one labeled 2b. "Ten inches."

Violet had memorized her multiplication facts up to twelve. In her notebook, she wrote down the three steps of the problem:

2a $5 \times 12 = 60$ in.
2b $10 \times 12 = 120$ in.
$120 - 60 = 60$ in.

Maybe if I do the math really fast, Nick won't notice, thought Violet. She did the problem in her head six more times and got the same answer. Then she copied the steps onto her worksheet. Nick and Ruby were done long before Violet. And Owen not long after Nick and Ruby. They all got 2b and 60 inches for the answer. Violet looked at Nick. He shook his head. Nick knew she was still doing the problem seven times. *Why is it so hard to fight the urge of sevens with math?* wondered Violet.

For the fifth and sixth questions, Violet, Nick, Ruby, and Owen took turns measuring three different dinosaur tracks. When they were finished with the worksheet, Violet made a bonus question for the group. That solved the problem of having a list of six in her field notebook. Violet added the last item:

7. Seven different dinosaur tracks measure 4, 5, 6, 7, 8, 9, and 10 inches. What's the total height of the seven dinosaurs if they're all standing on each other's heads?

$4 \times 12 = 48$ in.
$5 \times 12 = 60$ in.
$6 \times 12 = 72$ in.
$7 \times 12 = 84$ in.
$8 \times 12 = 96$ in.
$9 \times 12 = 108$ in.
$10 \times 12 = 120$ in.
$48 + 60 + 72 + 84 + 96 + 108 + 120 = 588$ in.

It's extra lucky that the seventh item on the list is a question with seven dinosaur tracks, thought Violet. She finished the problem right before Ms. Wishbone announced that it was time to move to the next center. But Violet didn't have time to check her answer.

"Well, what did you get?" asked Owen.

"It's okay if you didn't check the answer," said Nick. "Your math problem had a lot of parts to it."

Is it okay that I didn't check the answer? wondered Violet. She really wanted to do the problem seven times even though she knew it could make her OCD worse. Seven times just felt right. But she couldn't stay at this center and check her answer even if she wanted to. The rule was to go to the next center. It wasn't fair. But rules were rules.

"I bet you got it right the first time," said Ruby. Maybe she was right. Violet had taken her time with each step of the problem. She thought she had the right answer.

Violet stood up to move to the next center. "588."

Nick and Ruby smiled and nodded.

Owen held up his hand for a high five. Violet slapped it. Telling the group her answer before she was ready wasn't as bad as she thought.

CHAPTER 11

For the dinosaur trackways center, Violet had teacher time with Ruby and Nick in the reading nook. Ms. Daisy looked like an explorer ready to find dinosaur trackways. Her shirt had rolled-up sleeves that were buttoned to stay in place. Her pants could be zipped apart into shorts. Violet wished they were going outside on a real adventure.

The wooden structure surrounding the large window made it feel closer to the outdoors. Ms. Wishbone said the reclaimed wood had been a barn before it became a reading nook. Binoculars hung next to the large window to view wildlife. Violet had seen a lot of deer, squirrels, and birds from this spot. Nick even saw a turkey last month. Too bad Violet couldn't see real dinosaurs out the window. But at least she could talk about them at school today.

Violet started a new list in her field notebook:

Center #2
Dinosaur Trackways

"We're going to start by creating our own dinosaur tracks." Ms. Daisy pointed to the mounds of brown, green, and blue clay and the stamps in the center of the table. "Each of you should choose a different color of clay. And use the stamp next to it to mold the clay into a dinosaur track. We have a stamp for a theropod, an ornithopod, and a sauropod. But it's your job to figure out which one you have."

The stamps molded their clay into different dinosaur track shapes. But Violet could never leave anything sticky on her hands. Neither could Ruby or Nick. Violet liked the gloves she got to wear when working with fossils. They kept the sticky clay at dig sites off her hands.

Ms. Daisy knew leaving traces of clay on their hands would be a problem. "You can wash your hands when you're done," she said.

Violet, Nick, and Ruby took turns at the sink. They returned to the table to study their clay dinosaur tracks.

"Violet, do you know what kind of dinosaur made your track?" asked Ms. Daisy.

"A theropod," Violet said.

"How do you know?" asked Ms. Daisy.

"Theropods were meat-eating dinosaurs that walked on two legs," Violet said. "They had a V-shaped track

with three long, bird-like toes ending in claws. Some theropods had a really small toe on the side too. But this track doesn't have it."

"Wonderful," said Ms. Daisy.

In her field notebook, Violet summarized what she had said in three items.

"What about you, Nick?" asked Ms. Daisy. "Do you know what kind of dinosaur made your track?"

"An ornithopod," said Nick. "It usually has three short and thick toes. But its track is more rounded than a theropod's track."

Nick's answer gave Violet two more items for her list. That made five total.

"And how about you, Ruby?" asked Ms. Daisy.

"A sauropod," said Ruby. "It makes a large, wide track that looks almost like a circle. It's hard to see the toes and claws in the track. But a sauropod has five toes and usually three claws."

It sounded like she said "sarpod" and "quaws." But Violet knew what she meant. Ruby had trouble when she said longer words because of her dyslexia. And it was hard for her to say words that started with "cl" too.

Violet put the information about sauropods in two items. That made a complete list of seven.

"Great answer!" said Ms. Daisy. "It looks like the sauropod track we saw at the natural history museum, doesn't it?"

Ruby nodded.

"Are we ready for our next dinosaur detective job?" asked Ms. Daisy. "We're going to study trackways like ichnologists." She pointed to the dinosaur track stickers covering the window. Each trackway was a different color of the rainbow. *Perfect*, thought Violet. *Seven trackways!*

Ms. Daisy handed them each a worksheet. The top half of the page was for observations and the bottom half for conclusions.

Ms. Daisy pointed to the top half with her pencil. It had a triceratops-head eraser topper that tapped the paper. "Here, write what you notice about the dinosaur trackways," said Ms. Daisy. "For example, what do the tracks look like? How far apart are they? How many tracks are there?"

She hit the bottom half of the worksheet with the triceratops eraser. "And here, write your conclusions about what the trackways mean. For example, what kind of dinosaurs made them? Were the dinosaurs in the spot at the same time or different times? Were they walking or running?"

Violet studied the twists and turns of the dinosaur trackways. She knew what could've happened to make them. But she wasn't sure. How could she decide? What if she was wrong? Ms. Daisy would be grading the worksheet. It needed to be perfect.

She wrote on her worksheet:

The sauropod

But she erased it. She tried again. And added some words:

The sauropod trackway overlaps with

No, "overlaps" isn't the right word, thought Violet. She erased it. She erased the rest of the words too.

The sauropod and theropod dinosaurs probably went on these trackways at the same time, she thought. But she didn't know how to explain this. She stared out the window at a deer near the edge of the woods. As if it would help her come up with the perfect words. She rubbed her baby *T. rex* tooth seven times. But nothing was working.

Ruby didn't put her answers on the worksheet. She typed her answers on her tablet instead. Ruby needed extra help with writing because she was dysgraphic. Writing by hand was hard for her. Her tablet underlined the words that she spelled wrong. And if Ruby started to type a word, her tablet would show her a small list of words that it could be. Then, she would pick the word she wanted to use from the list.

Nick doodled dinosaur comics with trackways on his worksheet. But at least he had words. Captions, speech bubbles, and thought bubbles. Violet had nothing. She took a deep breath in, counting to seven. She blew a deep breath out, counting to seven.

"Do you want to talk more about the tracks, Violet?" asked Ms. Daisy.

Violet shook her head. *Will Ms. Daisy think I don't know anything about dinosaur trackways?* she wondered. Violet flipped through her field notebook. She knew so much about dinosaurs. Why couldn't she do this? "I know what I want to say, but I don't know how to put it in words on the worksheet."

"If you start writing down what you notice about the dinosaur tracks," said Ms. Daisy, "the words will come to you. The answers on the worksheet don't have to be perfect sentences as long as you get your ideas across."

Violet knew Ms. Daisy was right. Anytime Violet wrote some words, more words did come to her. But it didn't work if she erased the words and had to start over. She had to keep going. On her worksheet, Violet rewrote:

The sauropod trackway

Then she added:

meets the theropod trackway. The sauropod trackway stops. The theropod trackway continues. It looks like the predator attacked the prey.

Ms. Daisy looked over Violet's shoulder at the worksheet. "Very good!"

Violet let the words pour out onto her worksheet. Now she was getting somewhere. The worksheet didn't have to be perfect. A paleontologist or ichnologist didn't write perfect notes the first time they saw tracks. And Violet didn't have to either.

CHAPTER 12

On Tuesday after school, Violet tested the magic mirror at the natural history museum. She had help from the other fourth graders and Matt in the club.

The magic mirror was in a large room that branched off from the Jurassic Atrium. The room had walls on three sides and a view of towering sauropods on the open end. Violet turned to the Jurassic Land exhibit section in her field notebook. She started a new entry:

December 11
Natural History Museum
Magic Mirror Test #3
Allosaurus fragilis on the Hunt

"This is going to be like nothing you've ever seen before," said Violet.

"Awesome!" said Nick.

"We're going to start with the third scene out of seven," said Violet. "This one is extra special. In the

Jurassic Atrium, the dinosaur bones are lined up to show how *Allosaurus fragilis* threatened the sauropods and stegosaur. And the mural around the atrium adds more of these dinosaurs to the scene. With the magic mirror, the scene comes to life. These dinosaurs interact with each other and with you."

"So how does it work?" Connor pointed to the huge screen on the wall.

"It's a smart screen," said Violet. "All you have to do is stand in front of the magic mirror. And I'll start it."

"Easy enough," Ruby said.

"Enjoy the experience while you're in it," said Violet. "After we're done watching, we'll make a list of what we think should be kept, taken out, and added."

"Bring it on!" said Connor.

Ruby put one foot in front of the other like she was lining up for a race.

"Show me what you got," said Matt.

Jasmine flapped her hands. "But what about photos?" asked the voice on her tablet.

"Oh, you're going to love this," said Violet. "The magic mirror is set to take photos and a video of us with the dinosaurs. I'll make sure everyone gets a copy."

"Welcome to Jurassic Land!" Violet pushed the touch buttons on the large screen. She selected the scene for *Allosaurus fragilis* on the hunt.

The club kids appeared on the screen with monkey puzzle trees towering over them. These trees could grow up to 150 feet tall. *They're huge!* thought Violet. The dark green leaves covered the curved branches like scales. Dad said the sharp leaves were like armor. They made it harder for dinosaurs to eat monkey puzzle trees.

The whistling wind was strong enough to sway the monkey puzzle trees. Violet thought she could feel the cool wind on her face. She stretched her neck up high. Heavy cones swung back and forth on the top branches of the monkey puzzle trees.

The sauropods entered the scene. *Apatosaurus* mom and baby and Dippy stomped up to the monkey puzzle trees. The mom broke off leaves for the baby. *Stegosaurus armatus* joined a herd of *Stegosauri* making their way to the trees too. Their cherry-red plates stood out against the dark green landscape.

Thump. Thump. Thump.

"Where is that noise coming from?" Ruby whispered.

Violet whipped her head around. *Allosaurus fragilis* charged ahead. Ruby and Matt backed away slowly.

Violet put her hand in the air to signal to stop. Ruby and Matt froze. Nick, Jasmine, and Connor did too.

Apatosaurus mom turned her head to look behind her. The predator was hunched over with its razor teeth opened wide and ready to attack. Violet spotted another packmate off in the distance but coming right toward them. She pointed to show her club friends.

"That predator isn't really going to eat mom or baby, right?" Ruby whispered to Violet.

Violet shrugged. She didn't know any more than Ruby how the scene would play out. This was the first time Violet was testing it too.

Dippy backed away from *Apatosaurus* mom and baby. Dippy bumped into the long, pointy snout of *Camptosaurus aphanoecetes*. This duck-billed herbivore dinosaur that walked on two feet looked like it had a beak.

Dippy smacked a monkey puzzle tree with his tail. The loud cracking noise sounded like a whip. *Does Dippy think it's an attack from behind?* wondered Violet. Cones were knocked loose from the tallest tree branches. They were as big as watermelons and weighed as much as them too!

"Heads up!" Matt warned the others. He hunched down with his hands on his head.

The club kids ducked and covered their heads with their hands. On the screen, one cone brushed the side of Jasmine's head and landed a few inches from her feet.

"Whoa!" said Violet. "That was a close one."

A cone hit one predator in the face. Another cone struck the other predator on its back. They grunted and groaned.

While the cones dropped, Dippy stomped away. *Apatosaurus* mom and baby escaped. The herd of *Stegosauri* moved on. Both *Allosauri* retreated.

Violet turned off the magic mirror. Dad had really outdone himself with the monkey puzzle trees. She had known he would add them to the library of plants for the magic mirror. But she wasn't expecting watermelon-sized cones to drop on the scene. *How cool is that!* thought Violet.

She was still trying to convince Mom to let her have a monkey puzzle sapling in her room. Dad had some saplings in the greenhouse. Somehow, she didn't think the magic mirror scene of cones dropping from the sky was going to help her case.

Violet sketched the scene in her field notebook. Dippy and stegosaurs parading onto the scene. *Apatosaurus* mom protecting her baby from predators. And the cones

dropping from the monkey puzzle trees that made the predators lose their focus.

The drawing of *Apatosaurus* baby wasn't quite right. Violet erased it with her Stegosaurus eraser. Her next attempt was better. But not good enough. The club was waiting for her. And they had four more tests to do. She would have to fix the sketch later.

"I'll start the list in my field notebook," said Violet. "Let me know what you think should stay in the scene."

Jasmine typed. "That giant cone almost hit my head," said the voice on her tablet, "but the trees should stay."

In her field notebook, Violet wrote the first item under the drawing for *Allosaurus fragilis* on the hunt:

1. Keep monkey puzzle trees with giant falling cones

"Definitely," said Nick. "I got one to keep too. *Apatosaurus* mom really looked like she was protecting her baby from the predators."

Violet wrote another item on the list:

2. Keep head of Apatosaurus mom swung to one side to look toward the predators

"I really liked the *Stegosaurus*," said Ruby. "It looked

clueless about the danger." Violet added another item to the list:

3. Keep Stegosaurus joining its herd near the dangerous predators

"I wasn't expecting another predator to come along," said Matt. "Definitely a keeper." Violet wrote:

4. Keep Allosaurus packmate that joins the scene to double the trouble

"Okay, so now what would you add or change?" asked Violet. "I'll start. Dippy would have had to knock the trees really hard to get the cones to fall like that." Violet added in her field notebook:

5. Change so Dippy panics when he bumps into Camptosaurus and swings his tail harder

"Yeah, that duck-billed dinosaur was right behind Dippy," said Connor. "It was probably trying to take cover from the predator. But the duck-billed dinosaur looked like it was just standing there." Violet wrote another item on the list:

6. Add Camptosaurus ducking for cover behind Dippy

Dad popped his head into the room. "Did you like the monkey puzzle trees?"

"I loved them!" said Violet. *Was he waiting around the corner just so he could ask me?* she wondered.

"It almost smashed my head!" Jasmine typed on her tablet, and then the voice said it out loud.

Dad smiled. "I did my best to make the plants come alive."

"I know what to add!" Bo leapt into the room. Luke joined him. And then Lao Lao. She must have brought them. *Did they have to come in now?* thought Violet. She had more work to do on the magic mirror. Violet's eyes met Lao Lao's. Violet imagined Lao Lao telling her to be nice to Bo.

Bo flapped his arms really wide like he was flying. "We should put pterosaurs in the magic mirror." He jumped up and down with Luke.

"You mean the flock of *Cynorhamphus suevicus*?" said Violet. The pterosaurs hung from the Jurassic Atrium ceiling about thirty feet above the ground.

"What a great idea!" said Dad.

"Pterosaurs are so cool!" Jasmine's tablet said.

"Flying dinosaurs would be great," said Ruby.

"They're not dinosaurs," said Violet. "They're flying reptiles."

"But still really cool," said Connor. "They look like they have swan beaks."

"Their wings are bigger than my arms." Bo stretched his arms wide.

"That's right, Bo," said Lao Lao. "*Cynorhamphus* has a six-foot wingspan."

"They could swoop down at the crowd on opening night," said Nick.

"Awesome!" said Matt.

Violet had to admit it wasn't a bad idea. The Jurassic Land exhibit was on dinosaurs. But if Jurassic plants were part of it, why not flying reptiles too? "Okay, I'll put it on the list," said Violet. She wrote in her field notebook:

7. Add a flock of Cynorhamphus swooping down

Maybe Bo wasn't so bad at coming up with good ideas for the magic mirror after all. Violet checked off *Allosaurus fragilis* on the hunt from her list of seven magic mirror scenes. *Four more tests to go*, she thought. *The exhibit is going to be amazing!*

CHAPTER 13

On Friday, Violet was so anxious that something would go wrong with the new exhibit. She could barely focus on school all day. She wanted to be at the museum, checking to make sure that everything was ready for opening night. But Mom had made her go to school.

Lao Lao picked up Violet, Nick, Grace, and Bo after school to take them to the museum. The rest of the club would come when the exhibit opened.

At the museum, Violet walked around with Nick for a final check of the augmented reality stations in the Jurassic Atrium. They stopped in front of *Stegosaurus*.

"What if something goes wrong?" Violet picked up one of the tablets from the docking station.

"But we checked the exhibit every night this week." Nick took another tablet from the docking station. "What's the worst thing that could happen?"

"Do you really want to know?" asked Violet. Nick had asked a question like this before. And he knew about her intrusive thoughts. He should know by now that she would imagine the worst to be really bad.

"Oh, sorry," said Nick. "I shouldn't have asked that. I know you can't control the bad thoughts. But we've checked the exhibit with the club so many times. And of course, your parents and the rest of the people at the museum have too."

"I know, but I still want to check the exhibit seven times myself before it opens."

"You told me to let you know when you were letting your OCD take over," said Nick. "Checking the exhibit seven times now would definitely count. Besides, we have to eat dinner too." Violet had forgotten that Mom had invited Nick and Grace to eat takeout food with her family at the museum before the exhibit opened.

Violet scanned the QR code and held the tablet next to the bones of *Stegosaurus*. Nick scanned the QR code too. On her tablet, the tiny head of *Stegosaurus* with a thick neck and body appeared. Its pentagon-shaped plates like kites changed from green to red. Its honeycomb-shaped scales covered its body. And its tail with spikes in it swung through the air. *Stegosaurus is perfect*, thought Violet.

But then the dinosaur suddenly disappeared from Violet's tablet. It had turned off. Violet hit the power button to turn the tablet back on, but it wouldn't restart. "That's strange," she said. "The tablet isn't working." Violet took in a deep breath and counted to seven. She let it out, counting to seven too.

Nick still had *Stegosaurus* on his tablet. But a message flashed on the screen: "Low battery."

"Look!" Nick pointed to the battery symbol in the upper right-hand corner of the tablet. It said 5 percent. But the tablet should've been fully charged. Something wasn't right.

"Let's check the other docking stations." Violet rubbed her baby *T. rex* necklace seven times. *This can't be happening*, she thought. *The tablets worked fine yesterday*.

Violet and Nick split up to check the battery power on all the tablets around the Jurassic Land exhibit. The rest of the tablets were fully charged and ready to go.

What's wrong with the Stegosaurus docking station? thought Violet. None of the tablets were charged on this docking station. It wasn't a problem with just one tablet.

Why would the tablets on this docking station have a problem but not the other ones? wondered Violet. Maybe the docking station had a problem. Violet followed the

cord running down from the docking station to the power strip. It was plugged in. Violet checked the outlet to make sure the plug for the power strip was all the way in. It *was* all the way in. *So now what?* wondered Violet.

She moved the docking station plug to another spot on the power strip. But the tablets didn't have the lightning bolt over the battery symbol. They still weren't charging. Violet tapped her hand on the docking station. She told herself that the tablets would charge if she tapped it seven times. But they didn't.

Nick checked to make sure the tablets were in the docking station the right way. They were perfectly placed in the slots.

Violet followed the cord again to the power strip. This time she noticed that the light on the power strip switch wasn't lit up. *That's it!*

"I see the problem." Violet flipped the switch on the power strip. The light on the switch turned orange. The tablets now had a charging icon in the upper right-hand corner. Violet breathed a sigh of relief.

"Nice catch!" said Nick. "No one would've been able to use those tablets for the opening tonight."

"And this is exactly why checking everything seven times is important," said Violet.

"But we found the problem after checking the tablets *one* time," said Nick. "And the opening still would've been great without them. The rest of the tablets at the other stations are fine. And there are extra tablets at docking stations at the front of the museum too."

"But opening night should be perfect," said Violet. "All the tablets should work."

"I know," said Nick. "I want my brick builds to be perfect too. But the augmented reality dinosaur exhibit isn't all on you—we're part of the team."

Nick looked around the room. Violet did too. Dad admired the plants. Mom rubbed her hand along the sauropod femur. Violet suspected that Mom rubbed it for good luck the same way she rubbed her *T. rex* necklace. Lao Lao, Bo, and Grace tested the magic mirror.

Maybe Nick was right. Violet wasn't the only one making sure everything was ready to go. Mom, Dad, and the rest of the museum people had been working on the exhibit for months. And the club, Bo, and Lao Lao helped every day after school this week too.

"The exhibit is fantastic," said Nick. "And everyone who comes to see it tonight is going to love it. Unless they don't like to have fun."

Violet laughed. "You really think so?"

"Absolutely," said Nick. "Where else can you go to see yourself on a big screen with dinosaurs? Dinosaurs that look real? Nowhere. This is the exhibit where everyone will go to see dinosaurs."

Everyone would come to this exhibit. And she wanted it to be absolutely perfect. But Violet knew it wasn't always possible to check everything seven times. She remembered what happened at school during the dinosaur math center. The center ended before she had time to check her answer on the math problem she had created. But it turned out okay.

Violet had taken her time with each step of preparing the dinosaur exhibit. She had worked hard on making sure everything was perfect. She took a deep breath in and counted to seven. And a deep breath out and counted to seven. She rubbed her baby *T. rex* tooth necklace. The exhibit was as ready as it was going to be. But would it be the big success that everyone expected?

CHAPTER 14

Ms. Daisy, the rest of the club, and their families started to arrive. And a lot of other people Violet didn't know. Mom and Dad roamed the exhibit in their Dippy T-shirts. Lao Lao and Bo wore theirs too. Violet and the rest of the club had on their Infinity Rainbow T-shirts. And Ms. Daisy wore her club T-shirt too.

Violet and Nick started the night in the fossil lab. Dr. Hart had already cracked the field jackets open earlier this week. It was too dangerous for Violet or Nick to handle the power tools needed to cut them open.

Next to them on the lab bench, Violet and Nick had dental picks and brushes. Nick slowly chipped away at the grayish clay speckled with bronze. It formed a solid layer around the grayish-white femur. Nick's mom waved at Nick and Violet from outside the lab. They waved back. Nick's mom must have just finished working.

Violet stared at the hatchling sitting in front of her on the lab bench. The clay was the only thing holding the 110-million-year-old fossils together. The bones were

beautiful. But she imagined herself picking up the dental pick and cracking the tiny bones.

She remembered what Mom said about her intrusive thoughts. They were just thoughts. She hadn't *really* broken the hatchling, and thinking about the tiny bones cracking wouldn't make them more likely to break either.

When the bad thoughts stopped, Violet imagined a different ending, a heroic story of her saving the hatchling from being destroyed. This is exactly what happened out in the field at Paleo Park. She was the one who saw the tiny bones when everyone else missed them. No one had taught Violet to imagine heroic stories.

One day, she decided that if she was going to have bad thoughts, then she wasn't going to let them end the story. She would be the heroine of her own story.

Thinking about herself as a heroine gave her the confidence and courage she needed. She grabbed the pick in her hand. Violet carefully removed the sticky gray clay around the whitish-gray bones.

Imagining herself as a heroine kept the unwanted thoughts away too. At least for now. She was determined not to let them get to her on opening night. The fossils were safe. She was more than capable of cleaning them. And that's exactly what she was going to do.

Violet and Nick sat in silence, slowly chipping and brushing away dust until they got to the surface of the bones.

"How long do you think it will take to clean this femur?" asked Nick.

"Probably five months or more, depending on how much time you spend on it," said Dr. Hart. "It's a big surface to clean."

"The hatchling is a lot smaller," said Violet. "But I have to work slowly because the bones are fragile. It will probably take me months to work on this too."

"I can tell you've done this before," said Dr. Hart.

Violet nodded. Their shift for the night in the fossil

lab was done. The femur didn't crack down in the middle like an earthquake. The hatchling bones didn't crumble. Cleaning the fossils was a success.

Violet and Nick left the fossil lab. The other kids who had found fossils at Paleo Park last weekend took their turn to show off their fossils. Bo brushed off a ginkgo leaf impression. Haley cleaned a tooth of *Dromaeosaur*. Matt worked on a crocodile tooth. Destiny brushed off a sequoia cone. And with Dr. Hart's help, Luke gently chipped away at a turtle shell.

Violet made her way through the Jurassic Atrium with Nick.

Dad pointed to the ferns, horsetails, club mosses, and other plants. "Every leaf and even the dirt on the ground was carefully planned for the Jurassic Land exhibit," he said to a small crowd gathered around him. Violet waved at Dad and kept moving with Nick across the room. They were on a mission.

In front of the Dippy skeleton, Mom told an excited crowd Dippy's story. She was on the part where she explained how the newspaper made up the colossal dinosaur story. Violet waved at Mom as she passed by.

Violet and Nick joined Connor, Jasmine, and Ruby at *Camarasaurus lentus*. They had planned to meet here when Violet and Nick finished cleaning their fossils for the night.

It was one of Violet's favorite dinosaur skeletons in the museum.

"I can't believe it's just a kid or maybe a teenager," said Connor.

The huge slab of sandstone hung on the wall with the dinosaur bones still stuck in it. "The bones were found out West," said Violet. "They came on a train in the bone bed that they were found in."

Camarasaurus had a small head with its jaw open and pointing upward. Its neck curved backward. Its tail curled up. The front legs were tangled together. And the back legs were twisted.

"It's called the death pose," said Violet. Leaving the dinosaur in the bone bed showed what position it was in when it died.

"That's creepy!" said the voice on Jasmine's table. She showed the group the skull and crossbones emoji at the end of the sentence she had typed.

But the dinosaur in a death pose came to life with augmented reality. It was a sauropod with the same small head, long neck, large body, and tree-trunk-sized legs as *Diplodocus* and *Apatosaurus*. But it wasn't as big as these sauropods, even as an adult.

"We can see how *Camarasaurus* died." Nick pointed to the bones.

"And imagine how it lived." Ruby pointed to her tablet.

After leaving *Camarasaurus* behind, Violet and Nick poked their heads into the room with the magic mirror. Lao Lao and Bo zigged and zagged in front of the scene of *Allosaurus* on the hunt. A flock of *Cynorhamphus* swooped down, just like Bo had wanted.

"Definitely better with pterosaurs," Nick whispered.

Watermelon-sized cones plunged from the top of the monkey puzzle trees. The audience ducked out of the way.

"It's a very different experience to be on the sidelines," whispered Violet.

***

Opening night at the natural history museum was a big success. No one wanted to leave when it was time to close for the night. Everyone wanted to come back. Visitors called the new exhibit "amazing," "unbelievable," and even "heart-stopping."

Nick told Violet that no one's heart had stopped

tonight. She let him know there was another meaning for the word—thrilling.

Violet and Nick's families and a few other museum workers were the only ones left in the building. Nick's sisters begged their parents to take them back to Paleo Park to look for more dinosaur fossils.

"The pterosaurs were great!" said Bo.

"It was an awesome idea," said Nick.

Lao Lao and Nick were right. Bo had good ideas for the Jurassic Land exhibit.

"Nick and I saw you in front of the magic mirror with the pterosaurs," said Violet to Bo. "They looked amazing."

"I can't wait to see the photos and video of Bo and Lao Lao from the *Allosaurus* on the hunt scene." said Mom.

"Me too," said Lao Lao. "The dinosaurs looked so real."

"And what about the plants?" asked Dad. "How did you like those watermelon-sized cones?"

"They almost knocked me out." Lao Lao laughed.

"That was my favorite part," said Violet. "And I still want a monkey puzzle tree . . ."

"I think we're going to keep the real ones in the greenhouse," said Mom.

It was worth a try, thought Violet.

"You know, Bo," said Violet, "we can use the museum app on my tablet again this weekend."

"Yeah!" Bo jumped up and down. "I want to see the rest of the dinosaurs from the tree house."

Violet turned toward Nick. "Do you want to see Jurassic dinosaurs stomping through the woods in our backyard?"

"Count me in," Nick said.

"Before we go, I want to show you something in the Cretaceous room," said Violet to Nick. "We'll be right back," she said to Mom. Violet and Nick walked to the next room in the museum.

Some of Violet's and Nick's favorite dinosaur bones were in the Cretaceous room. They had spent hours staring at the bones, just like Violet had done with Lao Lao.

In the middle of the room, two *T. rex* fought over *Edmontosaurus*. Mom said the museum staff had a nickname for this duck-billed dinosaur—Dead Ed.

"What would the magic mirror scene of two *T. rex* battling it out over Dead Ed look like?" said Violet.

"Now that would be a fun scene to test," said Nick. "Dead Ed would be ripped to shreds. And maybe the *T. rex* would get bored with him and go after the audience instead. It would definitely be heart-stopping." Nick laughed.

"Are you going to help with the Cretaceous Land exhibit too?" Violet asked.

"Sure," said Nick. "We can work as a team to check the exhibit."

"And I can count on you to remind me that checking the exhibit should be a team effort?"

"You bet," said Nick. "We're in this together."

Violet smiled. She couldn't wait to do it all over again. The Jurassic Land exhibit was a big success. The Cretaceous Land exhibit would be too. And Violet would continue to be the heroine of her own story.

JEN MALIA is an associate professor of English and the creative writing coordinator at Norfolk State University. Originally from Pittsburgh, Jen currently lives in Virginia Beach with her husband and three kids. Jen has written for the *New York Times*, the *Washington Post*, *New York Magazine*, *Woman's Day*, *Glamour*, *Self*, and others. Jen is the author of *Too Sticky! Sensory Issues with Autism*. Jen was diagnosed with ASD in her late thirties and has three neurodivergent kids with different combinations of ASD, ADHD, OCD, dyslexia, and dysgraphia.

PETER FRANCIS lives in England, where for over twenty years he has diligently created fresh, bright illustrations for both children's publishing and British television. His artwork is playful, thoughtful, and engaging. When not frantically sketching away, he explores castles, immerses himself in nature, paints, laughs, and (if time) sleeps!